Stella
the Star
Fairy

For Molly and Lizzie Barratt,
two special fairy fans

Special thanks to
Narinder Dhami

www.rainbowmagic.co.uk

ORCHARD BOOKS
338 Euston Road, London NW1 3BH
Orchard Books Australia
Hachette Children's Books
Level 17/207 Kent Street, Sydney, NSW 2000
A Paperback Original
First published in Great Britain in 2005
Text © Working Partners Limited 2005
Rainbow Magic is a registered trademark of Working Partners Ltd
Series created by Working Partners Limited, London W6 0QT
Illustrations © Georgie Ripper 2005
The right of Georgie Ripper to be identified as the illustrator
of this work has been asserted by her in accordance
with the Copyright, Designs and Patents Act, 1988.
A CIP catalogue record for this book is available
from the British Library.
ISBN 1 84362 869 4
10
Printed in Great Britain

Stella
the Star
Fairy

by Daisy Meadows

illustrated by Georgie Ripper

ORCHARD BOOKS

The Fairyland Palace

The Fairyland Christmas Tree

Wetherbury Village

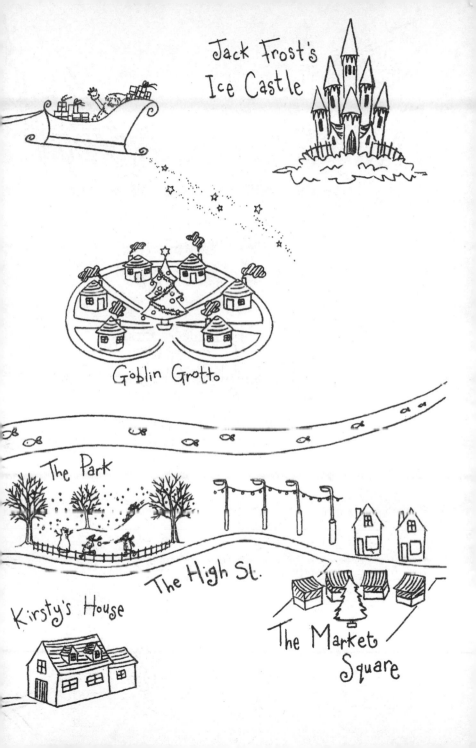

Christmas mischief I have planned,
So, goblins, go to Fairyland!
Find the fairy Christmas tree
Bearing magic items – three.

Steal these special decorations
To spoil all Christmas celebrations.
Candle, Bauble, magic Star –
Take them where no fairies are.

The Magical
Missing Candle

Contents

Darkness Falls

Mrs Tate popped her head round the door. "Are you ready, girls?" she asked. "It's time to leave for the Christmas Fair."

"Coming, Mum," Kirsty said, jumping up.

"I'm really glad I could come and visit," said Rachel Walker, as she

followed her best friend into the hall
to get their coats. Rachel had arrived
at Kirsty's house after the last day of
school term. Her parents were collecting
her on Christmas Eve.

"Me too," Kirsty replied. "You're
going to love the fair. And who
knows…we might even see
a Christmas fairy!"

Rachel and Kirsty thought they were the luckiest girls in the world because they had become friends with the fairies! Whenever the fairies were in trouble, they asked the girls for help – usually because cold, spiky Jack Frost was causing magical mayhem with the help of his nasty goblin servants.

"I forgot to tell you!" Kirsty said, pulling on her boots. "Every year someone from my school is chosen to be the fair's Christmas King or Queen, and this year it's my friend Molly."

"Wow! I bet she's really excited," said Rachel smiling. "I'd love to be Christmas Queen!"

Kirsty nodded as her parents
joined them.

"Everybody ready?" said Mrs Tate.
"Then let's go..."

"Has someone turned the Christmas
tree lights off?" Mr Tate asked. "They
were on a few minutes ago, but
they're off now."

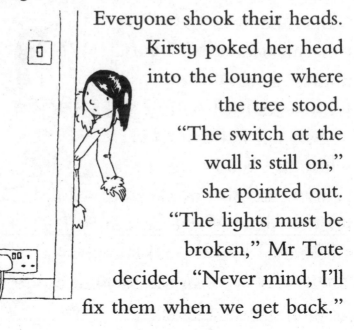

Everyone shook their heads.
Kirsty poked her head
into the lounge where
the tree stood.
"The switch at the
wall is still on,"
she pointed out.
"The lights must be
broken," Mr Tate
decided. "Never mind, I'll
fix them when we get back."

"Yes, we must go," Kirsty's mum agreed. "The parade starts soon."

Quickly, they left the house and walked up Twisty Lane towards the high street and Wetherbury Market Square.

"I can hear music," Rachel said, looking excited.

Although it was a cold, frosty night, the square was packed with people bustling around stalls selling brightly-painted tree decorations, Christmas crackers, cakes and gifts. There was even an old musical organ playing a merry tune.

"It's great, isn't it?" Kirsty said, her
eyes shining. She pointed at a raised
platform in the middle of the square.
The Mayor of Wetherbury, in his
splendid robe and gold chain, was
standing there next to a large switch.
"And it'll be even better when the
Christmas Queen turns on the
illuminations," Kirsty added.

Rachel glanced around. She could
see dark shapes made of bulbs here
and there above their heads, but it
was hard to make out what the
shapes were. She was looking forward
to seeing them all lit up.

"Ooh, I can't wait to see
Molly!" Kirsty exclaimed, as the
parade began.

The first float that rumbled into the square was Santa's workshop, with elves making toys and Santa sitting on a golden sleigh.

"Oh, look!" Rachel gasped, as another float came into view, carrying a huge papier-mâché Christmas pudding with a sprig of holly on top. Several more floats followed, all looking wonderfully colourful and Christmassy.

"Here's Molly," Kirsty said to Rachel as the final float appeared. "Doesn't she look pretty?"

Kirsty's friend was dressed in white and silver. Her dress had a long full skirt, scattered here and there with sparkling snowflakes, and she wore a glittering silver tiara on her head. She sat on a jewelled throne, waving at the crowds. Behind her rose an ice palace, decorated with gleaming icicles.

19

Rachel nudged Kirsty. "The Christmas Queen's palace is much prettier than Jack Frost's gloomy ice castle!" she whispered, and Kirsty nodded eagerly.

The float drew to a halt next to the platform, and the mayor helped Molly up the steps as the crowd clapped.

"I would like to wish everyone in Wetherbury a very merry Christmas!" Molly announced. And then she pulled the switch with a flourish.

The square lit up in a dazzling blaze

of colour as the lightbulbs sprang to life. Everyone *oohed* and *aahed* as they gazed round at the illuminations above. "This is amazing!" Kirsty breathed. "It's beautiful," Rachel agreed. There were hundreds of snowflakes in different sizes strung on wires overhead, and they all glittered with rainbow-coloured lights. The Christmas Queen had come down from the platform now, and was waving at the two girls.

"Hi, there!" Molly called, her face glowing with excitement. "Did you like my float?"

"It was lovely!" Kirsty replied. "Molly, this is my friend, Rachel."

"Hi, Molly," said Rachel, admiring Molly's sparkling dress. "You look lovely."

"And these are definitely the best illuminations Wetherbury has ever had!" Kirsty added.

But just then, one of the snowflakes above their heads began to flicker. And as the girls glanced upwards, every single one of the beautiful snowflake illuminations suddenly flickered and went out.

Trouble in Fairyland

Everyone gasped in horror, including the girls.

"What's happened?" asked Kirsty. "They were fine a minute ago."

The mayor stood on the platform and called for everyone's attention. "Please don't worry," he said firmly, "we'll soon have the lights fixed.

And in the meantime, enjoy the fair."

"It's a shame about the illuminations," Molly said, "but I've had a brilliant evening!"

"I'm sure they'll be fixed by tomorrow," Kirsty replied.

"I hope so," Molly agreed. Then she smiled at the girls. "Now, I must go

and hand out presents to the children who were on the floats."

"A Christmas Queen's work is never done!" Kirsty said with a grin. Molly laughed and waved as she walked away.

Rachel and Kirsty turned back to Mr and Mrs Tate.

"What a pity the illuminations went out," said Kirsty's mum. "They looked so pretty."

"I'm glad I've only got to fix our tree lights and not all these bulbs!" said Mr Tate, smiling and shaking his head. "Let's go home and get warm."

As Mr and Mrs Tate walked on ahead, Kirsty turned to Rachel. "Isn't it dark tonight? There isn't a single star in the sky—" Suddenly she stopped dead, clutching her friend's arm. "Rachel, look!"

Rachel stared ahead.

The high street was lined with lamp-posts decorated with more of the snowflake illuminations, and the one closest to the girls contained a couple of lightbulbs that were shining brightly.

Kirsty looked puzzled. "How can those bulbs be on, when all the others aren't working?" she asked.

But Rachel didn't reply. Was she
imagining it or had she just seen a swirl
of glitter that looked like fairy magic?

"Rachel! Kirsty!" called a tiny,
musical voice.

"It's a fairy!"
Rachel gasped.

The fairy who
was fluttering
towards them,
blonde ponytail
bobbing, was
dressed in
Christmas green and red.
A string of sparkly gold fairy
lights was looped around the
waist of her little red dress, and
she wore a green feather boa around
her neck.

"Hello!" Kirsty said breathlessly as
the fairy landed lightly on her shoulder.
"What's your name?"

"I'm Stella the Star Fairy," the fairy
explained. "I'm in charge of all the
sparkly Christmas illuminations, the
fairy lights on Christmas trees and the
stars that guide Santa and his reindeer
on Christmas night!"

"Were you trying to turn the bulbs
back on?" asked Rachel curiously.

Stella's delicate, gauzy wings drooped
as she hung her head.
"I was," she sighed.
"But look!"
The girls glanced
up at the lamp-post.
The bulbs which Stella had
turned on had now gone out again.

"That's what happens every single time," Stella said glumly. "I turn a bulb on, but it just goes out again!"

"Don't worry, Stella," said Kirsty comfortingly. "They'll be fixed tomorrow."

But Stella shook her head. "No, you don't understand, Kirsty," she replied. "This is all Jack Frost's fault!"

"Jack Frost?" Kirsty repeated, glancing at Rachel. "Is he trying to spoil Christmas again?"

"Yes," sighed Stella. "You see, every year at Christmas-time we have a huge Christmas tree in Fairyland. There are three very special and magical decorations on it, but wicked Jack Frost sent his goblin servants to steal them, and now they're gone!"

"Oh, no!" Kirsty said. "Why are these decorations so special?"

"The first one is the shining white Candle," replied Stella. "It controls all the Christmas illuminations in the human world."

"So that's why the Wetherbury illuminations went out!" Rachel exclaimed.

Stella nodded. "The second is
the glittering Bauble. That controls all
the Christmas tree fairy
lights," she went on.

"Our tree lights!"
Kirsty gasped.
"That's why they're
not working."

"And the third is
the shining Star from
the top of the tree,"
Stella continued. "The Star makes sure
that the real stars shine in the night sky,
to guide Santa when he's delivering
presents. So we have to get all three of
the decorations back from the goblins
or Christmas will be ruined!"

"Do you know where the decorations
are?" Kirsty asked.

"Well, when we realised what the goblins were doing, we chased them," explained Stella. "So only the goblin with the magic Star made it back to Goblin Grotto. The others were forced to flee into the human world, taking the magic Candle and Bauble with them."

"Can we help find them?" asked Rachel.

Stella beamed at her. "I was hoping you'd say that!" she declared. "The Candle and the Bauble became bigger when they entered the human world, so they're big enough for you to spot."

"Then we'll look out for them," said Rachel in a determined voice. "We won't let Jack Frost spoil Christmas!"

"Thank you, girls!" cried Stella happily. "I'll rush back to Fairyland and tell the King and Queen that you're helping. Remember not to search too hard – the fairy magic will come to you!" And with a wave of her glittering wand, Stella flew away into the night.

Carols and Candles

"There isn't much time before Christmas," Rachel remarked, as she finished her cereal the following morning. "I hope we can get the Candle, the Bauble and the Star back by then."

"We'll do our best," Kirsty replied. "Mum says we can go Christmas

shopping in Wetherbury later, so
we can keep our eyes open for
fairy magic!"

After lunch the girls wrapped up
warmly and set off into town, leaving
Mr Tate struggling to fix the Christmas
tree lights. Although the sun was
shining in the pale blue sky, there was
a frosty chill in the air.

"Maybe we'll have some snow tonight," Kirsty said eagerly.

"Look," Rachel said, nudging her friend. "The electricians are trying to fix the illuminations."

Two men on top of long ladders were busy tinkering with the bulbs, as shoppers milled around in the street below.

"They won't have much luck unless we get the magic Candle back," Kirsty whispered.

The square was full of market stalls and busy shops. The floats and the platform from the previous evening were gone and a tall Christmas tree had been set up in their place. It was decorated with shiny baubles, tinsel and fairy lights, although the lights weren't working. A small group of children was gathered on one side of the tree, holding candles in silver holders and singing carols.

"Doesn't that sound Christmassy?"
Kirsty said with a grin, as the girls
walked closer to the sound of the
children's voices.

"Yes, but I think someone's singing
out of tune!" Rachel whispered
to Kirsty.

Kirsty nodded. She had noticed one
child who was a little
shorter than the
others. He was
muffled up in
a big coat with
a hood and a long
thick scarf, and he
was singing very
loudly but not very well.

"It's the one in the big coat,"
she whispered.

"He may not be able to sing very well," Rachel whispered back, "but he's got the best candle!"

Kirsty stared at the candle. It was bigger and rounder than the ones the other children were holding, and it was a very pure white colour which almost seemed to glow with hidden fire. Looking closely, Kirsty saw tiny white and silver sparkles swirl around the candle.

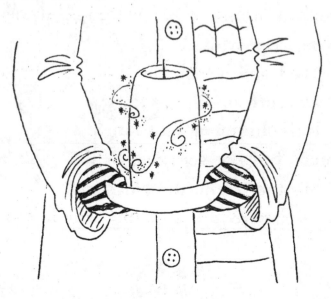

"Rachel, I think he's got the magic Candle!" Kirsty gasped. "He must be a goblin!"

Her heart thumping with excitement, Rachel stared at the carol-singer. As he moved, she just caught a glimpse of a green nose poking over the top of his scarf.

"It is a goblin!" she said to Kirsty. "But how are we going to get the Candle back?"

"Hello, Rachel!" a tiny voice sang out beside her.

Rachel jumped and turned to see Stella peeping out from behind a shiny bauble on the Christmas tree.

"I've spotted my magic Candle too!"

Stella whispered, as Rachel and Kirsty
gathered round the bauble to hide her
from view. "But I don't know how to
get it back. Any ideas?"

Rachel and Kirsty fell silent for
a moment, thinking. Then Kirsty's face
broke into a smile. "I've thought of
something that might work!" she said.
"Stella, could you magic up a copy of
the magic Candle?"

"Yes, I think so," she replied. "But it
won't be magical like the real Candle."

"That doesn't matter," said Kirsty, "as long as it fools the goblin."

"I'll do my best," Stella promised. She frowned in concentration and waved her wand. Immediately, green sparkles whizzed and fizzed around in front of her, and the copycat Candle started to take form.

A Sweet Trick

The green sparkles faded away and
a candle appeared in Kirsty's hand.
It was a perfect copy of the magic
Candle — except that it was pink!

"Oh, dear!" Stella laughed. "Let's
have another go."

She waved her wand again. This
time, as the sparkles died away, Rachel

and Kirsty watched the candle slowly
turn from pink to white.

"Perfect!" said Kirsty,
tucking the candle
into her pocket.
"Now, wait here."
Kirsty set off
across the square
while Rachel and
Stella kept an eye on the
goblin. When she came back she was
carrying two paper bags.

"What are those?" Rachel asked curiously.

"Sweets," Kirsty replied, opening the bags. Rachel peeped in and saw stripy mint humbugs in one bag and fruit sweets in coloured wrappers in the other.

"Now, you take these, Rachel," Kirsty said, handing the humbugs to her friend as the carol-singers finished their song. "And go and offer all the carol-singers a sweetie!"

Looking a bit puzzled, Rachel did as she was told. "Merry Christmas!" she said, holding the bag out to the singers nearest her.

"Oh, thank you!" they replied, each
taking a sweet.

Kirsty watched the goblin as Rachel
carried on handing out sweets. He was
looking very eager as he waited his
turn, but before Rachel reached him,
Kirsty stepped forwards. "Here, have
a sweet!" she said, holding out her bag.

Greedily the goblin thrust his gloved
hand into the bag and pulled out
a whole fistful of sweets. He didn't even

say thank you. But
then a look of
dismay came
over his face as
he stared at the
sweets in his
hand. Kirsty
grinned to herself.

The goblin had just realised that he couldn't unwrap his sweets and hold the Candle at the same time!

Rachel and Stella could now see what Kirsty's clever plan was.

"What's the matter?" Kirsty asked the goblin. "Don't you like sweets?"

"Yes, but I can't unwrap them while I'm holding this Candle!" the goblin grumbled.

Kirsty held out her hand. "Why don't you let me hold it for you?" she offered politely.

Rachel and Stella exchanged a hopeful look as they waited for the goblin to reply.

"Oh, no!" the goblin said quickly, his
eyes moving shiftily from side to side.
"This is a very special candle!"

"But I'll be standing right next to you
the whole time," Kirsty assured him.

The goblin still looked doubtful, so
Rachel decided to lend Kirsty a hand.
She took a sweet from Kirsty's bag
and unwrapped it right under the
goblin's nose. Then she popped it
into her mouth.

"Mmm!" she said. "These sweets are delicious!"

The goblin stared longingly at the sweets while Kirsty held her breath. Would he give in and let her take the Candle, or not?

Candlelight

After a moment, the goblin could
stand it no longer. "Here!" he said
gruffly, and he thrust the magic
Candle at Kirsty.

Kirsty took the Candle and breathed
a silent sigh of relief. Now that his
hands were free, the goblin started
unwrapping sweets as fast as he could.

Then he crammed them into his mouth,
all at the same time.

While the goblin was stuffing himself,
Kirsty quietly pulled out the fake
Candle. Quickly she swapped the two
candles over, and slipped the magic one
into her pocket.

"I'll have that back now," the goblin
mumbled through a mouthful of sweets.
He snatched the candle rudely from
Kirsty and turned his back on her.

Kirsty winked at Rachel and they moved over to the Christmas tree where Stella was hidden.

"Well done, girls!" the little fairy whispered, her eyes shining. "You've got the Candle!"

"And the goblin hasn't even noticed!" Kirsty laughed.

They all looked over at the goblin who was happily trying to sing through a mouthful of sweets.

"Let's take the Candle back to Fairyland where it belongs!" Stella said. While everyone was watching the carol-singers, she raised her wand and showered Kirsty and Rachel with fairy sparkles. The girls felt themselves shrinking to fairy size as they were whisked away in a swirl of magic dust.

A few moments later, the girls were flying over Fairyland with glittering, gauzy wings on their backs. Below, they could see red and white toadstool houses, and the fairy palace with a huge Christmas tree standing in front of it.

As Stella and the girls fluttered down towards the ground, they saw the King and Queen waiting to greet them.

"We have the magic Candle!" Stella announced.

"Kirsty and Rachel, welcome to Fairyland once more!" said King Oberon.

"And you have found our magic Candle," Queen Titania added happily. "We cannot thank you and Stella enough."

"We're glad to help," Kirsty said, and Rachel nodded.

59

Stella turned towards them. "Girls, would you like to put the Candle back on the tree?" she asked.

Both girls nodded and Kirsty took the Candle from her pocket. The branches of the tree were decorated with candles in silver holders, but the biggest and most beautiful holder was empty.

As Rachel held the branch steady, Kirsty carefully slotted the Candle into place. Immediately, it began to glow, giving off magical, fiery sparks.

"We'll do our best to find the Bauble and the Star, too," Rachel promised the King and Queen.

"Thank you," said Queen Titania
with a smile. "And now you must
return to Wetherbury and see how
beautiful it looks, thanks to you two
bringing the magic Candle home!"

She lifted her wand and
Rachel and Kirsty just
had time to wave
goodbye to Stella,
before they were
whisked away
in a swirl of
silver sparkles.

A moment later,
the girls found
themselves back in
Wetherbury square.

Nobody seemed to have noticed that
they'd vanished and reappeared again.

Everyone was too busy staring up at the Christmas illuminations, which were now working perfectly.

"Look, the goblin still hasn't realised he's been tricked!" whispered Kirsty.

The girls glanced at the goblin who was singing away happily, then joined the crowd of shoppers admiring the illuminations. Every single bulb was now alight, and the glittering snowflakes stood out brilliantly against the black velvet of the night sky.

Kirsty beamed at Rachel. "Aren't they beautiful?"

Rachel nodded. "We've made a good start," she said. "Now we've got to find the Bauble and the Star."

"Yes," Kirsty agreed with a smile. "But right now we'd better get on with our Christmas shopping, or our friends and families won't get any presents this year!"

"You're right!" Rachel laughed, and the two girls headed for the shops, the illuminations shining brightly overhead.

Snowballs and Baubles

Contents

A Snowy Start

"Kirsty! Wake up!"

Kirsty rolled over in bed. "What's the matter, Rachel?" she asked sleepily.

Rachel, who was at the window in her pyjamas, grinned at her. "It's snowing!"

"Really?" Fully awake now, Kirsty bounced out of bed and rushed over to the window. She peered out.

Great white flakes of snow were
drifting down from the grey sky.

"I hope it snows for ages," Rachel
said eagerly. "It would be brilliant to
have a white Christmas."

"Look, it's falling faster and faster,"
Kirsty pointed out.

The girls stood at the window, watching the snowflakes swirl, before they got dressed. The snow began to settle thickly on the lawn and flowerbeds in the garden, and showed no signs of stopping.

"If we get a lot of snow, we could go to the park after lunch and build a snowman," Kirsty suggested, as she brushed her hair.

"Ooh, that sounds great!" exclaimed Rachel. She was so excited, she almost lost her balance as she pulled on her jeans.

The girls went downstairs. In the
lounge, Kirsty's dad was on his hands
and knees tinkering with the Christmas

tree lights. Mrs Tate
was helping him.
"Morning,
girls," she said
with a smile.
Mr Tate
scratched his
head. "I don't
understand it," he
muttered, looking puzzled.
"We've checked the wiring and the
fuse is fine, but these fairy lights still
won't come on."

"Why don't you leave them now
and have some breakfast?" suggested
Kirsty's mum.

"Not yet," Mr Tate replied, frowning.
"I think I've almost got it..."

Smiling, Mrs Tate shook her head
and went off to the kitchen. Rachel and
Kirsty followed.

"The lights won't come back on until
the magic Bauble has been returned to
Fairyland," Kirsty whispered to Rachel.
"Maybe we'll find it today."

After breakfast, the girls spent the
morning wrapping Christmas presents.
But they kept an eye on
the weather. To their
delight, the snow fell
heavily all morning,
and by lunchtime
the back garden was
covered in a thick
white blanket.

After lunch, the girls slipped on their coats and boots. "Mum, can Rachel and I go to the park?" Kirsty asked. Mrs Tate nodded. "Make sure you're home in time for tea. Hopefully the fairy lights will be fixed by then," she added with a smile, "otherwise I'll have to start serving your dad his meals under the tree!"

Rachel and Kirsty laughed, and rushed out of the back door. They set off, stomping through the snow in their Wellies, and by the time they got to the park their cheeks were pink and glowing.

The park was full of people. Some
were building snowmen, others were
sledging and having snowball fights.
But Rachel and Kirsty quickly found
a quiet spot, not far from a group of six
children who were building a snowman.

"Let's make the body first," Kirsty
suggested, rolling a snowball in her
mittened hands. She put it on the
snowy ground and she and Rachel
began to roll it around so it got bigger
and bigger. Then they made a smaller
one for the head.

"See if you can find some pebbles,
Rachel," Kirsty panted, as she lifted the
snowman's head onto the top of his body.

Rachel rooted around in a flowerbed and managed to find a small handful of pebbles. She and Kirsty pressed the pebbles into the snowman, giving him eyes, a smiley mouth and four buttons down his chest.

"Isn't he handsome?" Kirsty said with a grin.

"Not without a nose!" laughed Rachel. "I'll look for a twig or something."

"Will this do?" called a silvery voice.
The girls spun round and stared up at
the sky. Stella the Star Fairy was flying
towards them, clutching a long thin
carrot in her arms.

"Perfect!" Kirsty agreed, as Stella
landed on the snowman's head. She
took the carrot from the fairy and stuck
it in the middle of the snowman's face.

"What are you doing here, Stella?" asked Rachel.

"Do you think the Bauble might be nearby?" added Kirsty eagerly.

Stella nodded and flew over to sit on Rachel's shoulder. "Look over there," she whispered, pointing to the group of children nearby. "And take a good look at that snowman!"

A Very Suspicious Snowman

Wondering what Stella meant, Rachel and Kirsty glanced over at the group of children, who had finished their snowman and were now having a snowball fight. The girls edged closer to the other snowman, staring at it curiously.

It wasn't like any snowman they'd seen before. For a start, it looked very mean.

It had a big nose made of a large, pointed stone, a grinning mouth of black pebbles and enormous feet of snow.

"It looks a bit like a snow goblin!" Kirsty said slowly. Then she gasped and pointed at the children. "And if that's a snow goblin, who are they?"

"Maybe they're Jack Frost's goblins in disguise!" Rachel whispered.

"Exactly!" Stella replied. "In which case, they might have the Bauble."

"I think we need to take a closer look," Kirsty said firmly.

Trying to keep out of sight, the girls made their way around the flowerbed and closer to the snowman. None of the children noticed them. They were too busy hurling snowballs at each other.

The girls peered at them, but they were so muffled up in hoods, scarves and coats that it was hard to tell if they were goblins or not.

As the girls watched, one of the
children was hit in the face by a large
snowball. With a screech of rage, he
tore his wet scarf away, revealing
a mean, green, warty face!

"They are goblins!" Kirsty exclaimed.
"I'll get you for that!" the goblin
yelled, shaking the snow from his big
nose and stamping his foot. "I'm going
to shove a snowball down the back of
your neck!"

"You'll have to catch me first!" the
goblin who had thrown the
snowball jeered.
He kicked lumps
of snow at the
other goblin,
then ran away
to hide behind
a tree, laughing
his head off.

"The Bauble
might be around here
somewhere," Rachel said
hopefully. "Maybe we should look
for it."

"We'll have to get a bit closer,"
Kirsty said, creeping forwards.

"Please be careful, girls," Stella
whispered anxiously.

Rachel and Kirsty began to edge towards the goblins, with Stella sitting on Rachel's shoulder and peeping out from under her hood. Snowballs were flying everywhere. As Kirsty, Rachel and Stella watched, a goblin wearing a red scarf threw a snowball so hard that he slipped and fell on his face.

"Ha ha ha!" the other goblins roared with delight.

Moaning and grumbling, the goblin scrambled to his feet. "Stop laughing at me!" he spluttered through a mouthful of snow. Then, as one of the laughing goblins bent to make another snowball, the goblin with the red scarf rushed over and shoved a snowball down the back of his blue coat.

"Arggh!" yelled the goblin in the blue coat angrily. "That's cold!"

"They're so covered in snow, they look like snow goblins themselves now!" Kirsty muttered, trying not to laugh. Rachel giggled, then covered her mouth with her hand; she didn't want the goblins to notice her.

Suddenly Kirsty frowned. "What's that goblin doing over there?" she whispered.

Until now, neither Stella nor the girls had noticed that one goblin was sitting on the ground, cross-legged, rolling snowballs. He had obviously decided that the best way to win the fight was to gather lots of snowballs in advance, and there was already a large pile of them beside him. As he carefully rolled another, a goblin in a woolly hat dashed over and tried to take the snowball from the top of the heap.

Looking furious, the sitting goblin dropped the snowball he was holding, and slapped the other's hand. "Make your own snowballs!" he shouted angrily, and instantly went back to rolling snowballs.

Kirsty looked at him a little more closely, and then nudged Rachel. "Look," she hissed.

Rachel looked and saw that in the goblin's lap was something round and sparkling, but it wasn't a snowball. It was pure white, even whiter than the snow, and it flashed and glittered

in the sunlight with every colour of
the rainbow.

"It's the magic Bauble!" Stella
whispered in delight.

Girls Under Fire

"It's beautiful!" Rachel sighed. "We must get it back."

"But how?" Kirsty murmured thoughtfully.

The girls and Stella watched the goblins, wondering how they could get hold of the Bauble. The sitting goblin was much more interested in snowballs than the Bauble, but he kept glancing up suspiciously to check that none of his companions was trying to steal from his snowball heap. That made it very difficult for the girls to get close to him without being seen.

Meanwhile the snowball fight was getting fiercer. The goblin in the blue  coat had hurried off to hide behind a tree and shake the snow out of his clothes. But the one in the red scarf sneaked around the other side of the tree, threw an armful of snow over his rival and then ran off to hide behind two other goblins.

Yelling with rage, the goblin in the blue coat gave chase and flung a big snowball at his enemy. Unfortunately, it hit the two other goblins and they shrieked with fury.

Now nearly all the goblins were covered in snow and ready to do battle.

They started taking sides – the goblin
in the red scarf and his two friends
against the goblin in the blue coat and
the one in the woolly hat.

"Hey!" the goblin in the red scarf
shouted to the sitting goblin, as he and
his team-mate were pelted heavily with
snowballs. "Come and help us! It's two
against three here!"

The sitting goblin
grinned and jumped
to his feet, not
realising that
as he did so,
the gleaming
magic Bauble
fell off his lap
and landed
softly on the
snowy ground.
He quickly scooped
up his snowballs and
ran to join the fight.

Rachel and Kirsty glanced at
each other.

"Let's try and grab the Bauble!"
Rachel whispered.

Kirsty nodded.

As the shrieking goblins hurled snowballs at each other, Kirsty and Rachel began to edge their way towards the Bauble. It lay there, sparkling prettily, but just as Kirsty was

about to stretch out her hand and pick it up, a large snowball suddenly hit her on the shoulder. "Stop them!" shouted a gruff goblin voice.

The girls had been spotted and, to their dismay, all six goblins were now running in their direction, flinging snowballs at them.

"Quick!" Rachel gasped, as one hit her on the arm. "Behind that tree!"

Forced to leave the Bauble where it was, Rachel and Kirsty dashed behind the tree as a huge shower of snowballs followed them.

"How are we going to get the Bauble back now?" Rachel panted. "We can't get past six goblins!"

"Wait!" Stella said suddenly. She
flew up to a branch of the tree, her
eyes shining. "I'll turn you girls into
fairies, and then we'll all be small
enough to dodge the snowballs!" she
declared happily.

"But if the goblins are throwing
snowballs at us, that means they know
we're there," Kirsty pointed out. "And
we don't want them to see us."

"Oh, yes, we do!" laughed Stella. "We want the goblins to see us and pelt us with snowballs!"

Kirsty and Rachel stared at Stella in amazement.

"How will it help to have lots of snowballs thrown at us?" asked Rachel.

"Trust me!" Stella told her with a cheeky grin. "My plan is going to work. I'm sure of it!"

A Daring Plan

Rachel and Kirsty had no idea what
Stella was up to, but they glanced at
each other and grinned. They both
loved being fairy-sized, so they waited
eagerly while Stella waved her wand
and scattered magic fairy dust over
them. A moment later they had shrunk
to the same size as their fairy friend and

fairy wings shimmered on their backs.

"Here we go!" Stella said,
fluttering out from behind the
tree. "Now make lots of
noise, girls, and make
sure the goblins see us!"

Still feeling puzzled,
Kirsty and Rachel
zoomed up into the
air behind Stella
and headed
towards the goblins.

"Yoohoo!"
Rachel called,
waving her arms.

"Over here!"
yelled Kirsty.

While Stella and the girls
had been behind the tree, the goblins

had clearly been stockpiling snowballs.
Now they looked up, and their
warty faces darkened with rage.
"Here come those
pesky fairies!" one
goblin shouted.
"Get them!"
snarled another.
All the goblins
began hurling
snowballs at Rachel,
Kirsty and Stella.
"This is scary!"
Kirsty panted as
a large snowball
whistled past her ear.
Now that she was
so tiny, the snowballs
seemed as big as houses.

"Well done, girls!" Stella called, as Rachel fluttered out of the way of another snowball. "Now, watch!"

As yet another snowball whizzed past

Stella, she lifted her wand and sprinkled magic fairy dust over it. Rachel and Kirsty watched curiously as the snowball changed in mid-air to become an exact copy of the magic Bauble.

"Look!" shouted the goblin in the blue coat furiously. "One of you just threw the Bauble instead of a snowball! What an idiot!"

"Who're you calling an idiot?" yelled
the goblin with the woolly hat,
beginning to throw snowballs at him
instead of at Stella and the girls.

"Stop it!" the first goblin panted,
dodging out of the way, "We have to
get the Bauble back!"

Arguing and grumbling, the six
goblins dashed after the fake Bauble,
which had fallen to the ground just
below Rachel, Stella and Kirsty.

"Keep those fairies away from the
Bauble!" shouted one of the goblins
and, as they ran, the goblins all began
hurling snowballs at Stella, Rachel and
Kirsty again.

"Can you see the real Bauble, girls?"
called Stella.

Rachel and Kirsty peered through
the hail of snowballs. The Bauble
had rolled to a stop near the edge
of the flowerbed.

"I see it!" Rachel shouted.

"Good," Stella replied, raising her
wand again. "You go and
get it while I give the
goblins something
else to chase!"

She waved her
wand and suddenly
the air was full of
magic sparkles.
This time, to
Kirsty and Rachel's
amazement, all
the snowballs flying
through the air turned
into fake Baubles.

"What's going on?"
yelled the goblin in the red
scarf, hardly able to believe his eyes.

He skidded to a halt as the baubles
began to fall to the ground around
him, and the other goblins banged right
into him so that they all ended up in
a snowy heap.

"Pesky fairies! Which is the real
Bauble?" one goblin spluttered as they
all began to scramble around picking
up the fake ones.

Meanwhile, Kirsty and Rachel were swooping down to the edge of the flowerbed.

"We'll both have to lift the Bauble now that we're fairy-sized," Kirsty panted as she landed on the ground. "And we'll have to do it quickly, before the goblins see what we're up to!"

Up, Up and Away!

Rachel and Kirsty both took hold of the Bauble.

"Now!" Rachel whispered.

Both girls fluttered their wings, struggling to fly upwards while lifting the Bauble. To their relief, it was just light enough for them to carry. Gradually the girls rose into the air,

113

higher and higher, until they were out
of the goblins' reach.

As Rachel and Kirsty hovered in
mid-air, holding the sparkling Bauble,
they saw the goblins down below.
They had given up searching, and
had started arguing instead.

"Who was the idiot that threw
the Bauble in the first place?" one of
them grumbled.

"Well, it wasn't ME!" another
goblin retorted.

"I bet it's YOUR fault!" the first
goblin shouted, prodding another in
the stomach.

"No, it's HIS fault!"
the prodded goblin
snapped, pushing
the goblin in the
woolly hat over.
With a howl
of rage, the
woolly-hatted
goblin tumbled
backwards into a deep
snowdrift and disappeared from view.

115

Immediately, the other goblins began pushing and shoving each other until they all ended up stuck in the snowdrift, their arms and legs waving frantically.

Meanwhile, a beaming Stella flew over to join Rachel and Kirsty. "We did it, girls!" Stella beamed, her eyes shining. "And now I think it's time we took the magic Bauble straight back to Fairyland."

She lifted her
wand and in a
whirl of green
sparkles, Rachel
and Kirsty were
whisked away,
the goblins'
grumbles ringing
in their ears.

As they flew over
Fairyland, Rachel and
Kirsty looked down to see
a large crowd of fairies waiting
around the Christmas tree by the royal
palace. Everyone looked very anxious,
but when they saw Stella, Rachel and
Kirsty flying towards them with the
magic Bauble, they clapped their
hands in joy.

117

"Thank you, thank you," cried
Queen Titania, coming to greet the
girls as they landed.

"Our precious Bauble is safely home
again," King Oberon declared, smiling.

"Rachel, Kirsty, would you put the
Bauble back on the tree for us?" Stella
asked sweetly.

"We'd love to!" Rachel and Kirsty
chorused, and they carried the Bauble
over to the tree.

There were baubles on every branch, except for a big one near the middle. Carefully the girls hung the Bauble on the branch, where it swayed gently, glittering and gleaming and sending flashes of rainbow colours here and there.

"We left the goblins stuck in a snowdrift!" Stella told the King and Queen with a grin.

"They were arguing so much, it'll take them ages to dig themselves out!" Kirsty added.

Everyone laughed, but then Queen Titania sighed.

"Stella, Rachel and Kirsty," she said solemnly, "you have done very well to return the Candle and the Bauble.

But the last decoration, the Star, is the most important of all!"

"Why?" Rachel asked.

"Because without the magic Star, the stars will not twinkle in the night sky," the Queen explained. "And without the stars, Father Christmas can't find his way to deliver the presents on Christmas Eve."

"You mean nobody will get any presents?" gasped Kirsty.

The Queen nodded.

"And Christmas Eve is tomorrow," Rachel said. "We don't have much time left!"

"At least we know where the Star is,"
Stella pointed out. "It's hidden
somewhere in Goblin Grotto."

"Then we'll have to go there and get
it back!" Kirsty said in a determined
voice. "Can you take us Stella?"

The little fairy nodded solemnly.

"We won't let you down,"
Rachel told the King
and Queen firmly.

"Thank you,"
Queen Titania
replied. "And now
I think you both
deserve a good rest.
Go home, and forget all
about the goblins until tomorrow."

The two girls said their goodbyes
as the Fairy Queen waved her wand.

In a swirl of fairy dust, the girls were swept up and carried home. They landed gently on Kirsty's front doorstep.

"We must find the Star tomorrow, Kirsty," Rachel sighed.

"Yes," Kirsty agreed. "Christmas just won't be Christmas without Santa."

Suddenly, Rachel pointed at the window of the lounge. "Look, Kirsty!" she said, smiling all over her face. "Your Christmas tree fairy lights are working again!"

"Hurrah!" Kirsty cried happily.

The two girls rushed inside.

Mr Tate was sitting on the sofa, looking very pleased with himself. "Well, I fixed the lights, girls," he announced. "It was just a matter of changing every bulb on the string."

Rachel and Kirsty smiled at each other.

"That's what Dad thinks," Kirsty whispered.

"But we know better!" Rachel added.

Search for
the Star

Contents

Girls Become Goblins!

"I wonder what Goblin Grotto is like," Rachel said, excitedly. It was Christmas Eve, and she and Kirsty were out in the Tates' back garden, sweeping the snow off the paths. "Do you think it'll be scary?"

"I hope not!" Kirsty replied with a laugh, brushing away the last heap of snow.

"But don't forget, we'll have Stella
there with all her lovely fairy magic to
help us!"

Rachel grinned and nodded. "But
how will we get the Star without
the goblins seeing us?" she went on.
"I mean, even if we're fairy-sized,
there's still a chance we'll be spotted."

"I know," Kirsty agreed. "But it's not
going to stop us from trying, is it?"

"Of course not!" Rachel said in a determined voice. "We have to get the Star back or there will be no real stars in the night sky to guide Santa when he's delivering presents!" Then she shaded her eyes and gazed across the garden. "Kirsty, look at that cute little robin."

Kirsty looked where Rachel was pointing. A robin was bobbing through the air, coming straight towards them.

"There's something on its back," Kirsty said in surprise.

"Hello, girls!" called a tiny, silvery voice.

"It's Stella!" Rachel gasped.

The fairy was riding along on the robin's back, waving at Rachel and Kirsty. The little bird landed on the fence, and Stella hopped off. She patted the robin's head, and it flew away into a nearby tree.

"Are you here to take us to Goblin Grotto?" asked Rachel.

Stella nodded. "Are you sure you want to do this, girls?" she asked, her face very serious.

"Of course we do!" Rachel
replied firmly.

"But we're a bit worried about
getting spotted by the goblins," Kirsty
added. "We need some sort of disguise."

"Oh!" Rachel exclaimed suddenly.
"Maybe we could disguise ourselves
as goblins!"

"That's a great idea!"
Kirsty agreed eagerly.
"Could you make
us goblin-sized
and green, Stella?"

"Oh, yes!" the
fairy laughed.

"Then if we wrap our
scarves around our faces and
put up our hoods like the goblins
have been doing, no one will

notice us!" Rachel declared happily.

"Here goes, then," Stella cried, and she waved her wand, sending sparkling fairy dust spinning all around the girls. Immediately they shrank down to the size of goblins.

"Am I green?" asked Kirsty. Then she caught sight of Rachel's face and burst out laughing. Her  friend was as green as the greenest goblin! Rachel was laughing too hard at Kirsty's emerald-coloured face to answer.

"You're both green all
over!" Stella said with
a smile, as the girls
took off their gloves
and laughed again
at their green fingers.
"There's just one problem
though," she went on with a frown.
"My magic can't make you look mean
and nasty like the goblins. So you'll
have to do that yourselves."

Kirsty and Rachel were still giggling
at each other's strangely coloured faces.

"Try to look as angry and grumpy as
you can," Stella told them.

Rachel and Kirsty managed to stop
laughing, and Rachel screwed up her
face into a frown, while Kirsty scowled
and narrowed her eyes.

"Not mean and nasty enough," Stella declared. "Try again."

This time both girls hunched their shoulders and screwed up their faces into the ugliest, grumpiest frowns they could manage.

"Well, you don't look quite as nasty as real goblins," Stella laughed, "but it'll have to do!"

"Let's wrap ourselves up well,
Rachel," Kirsty said. "That will help
to hide our faces."

Quickly the girls wound their scarves
around the lower part of their faces and
pulled up their hoods.

"Now," Stella went on, "are you
ready to come with me to Goblin
Grotto, my goblin friends?"

Both girls nodded eagerly, and with
a flick of Stella's wand and a shower of
magic sparkles, they were on their way!

Starshine in Goblin Grotto

Seconds later, in a whirl of fairy magic, Stella, Rachel and Kirsty arrived at Goblin Grotto. The two girls had never been there before, and they stared around curiously.

The goblins lived in small wooden huts which were dotted here and there around the foot of a snow-covered hill.

Smoke curled from the chimneys of
all the houses. The ground was covered
with thick snow and ice, and the sky
overhead was grim and grey with no
sign of the sun. In the distance, at the
top of the hill, Rachel and Kirsty could
see Jack Frost's ice castle. A cold, grey
mist drifted around its frozen blue
turrets.

"Brr," whispered
Kirsty, wrapping
her arms round
herself. "It's even
colder here than
it is at home!"

Rachel, who was
closest to one of the

wooden huts, peered cautiously through
the window. A fire was burning merrily
in the hearth, and a goblin was
slumped in an armchair in front of it.
He was stretching out his toes to the
flames, and mumbling under his breath.

"Oh, my feet are frozen!"
he complained.

Rachel smiled. "Look," she whispered
to Kirsty. "I'd forgotten how much
goblins hate to have cold feet."

Kirsty peeped through the window and grinned.

"Girls!" Stella gasped, tapping Rachel on the shoulder. "Someone's coming!"

Suddenly feeling very scared, Rachel and Kirsty spun round. A big goblin with a wart on the end of his nose was tramping down the snowy track towards them.

"Quick, Stella!" Kirsty said urgently. "Hide!"

"All right," Stella whispered. "But put on your grumpiest faces, girls."

The fairy fluttered out of sight behind the wooden hut, and Kirsty and Rachel screwed their faces up into ugly frowns. Hearts thumping madly, they waited as the goblin came closer. Would he realise that they were humans in disguise, and not goblins at all?

As the goblin passed by, he threw the two girls a grumpy look. "What are you staring at?" he snapped.

Rachel and Kirsty didn't reply, and the goblin trudged on his way.

Both girls sighed with relief.

"Our disguise worked!" Kirsty breathed.

"Well done, girls," Stella said, flying out from behind the hut. "Now we must find the Star!"

Rachel's face fell. "But how are we going to find it?" she asked. "We can't search the houses if there are goblins inside them."

Kirsty nodded thoughtfully and gazed around. Suddenly her eyes opened wide. "Actually, I don't think *finding* the Star is going to be a problem," she said. "But getting it down might be!"

Rachel and Stella looked puzzled.

"What do you mean, Kirsty?" asked Rachel.

"Look," Kirsty replied, pointing down the track.

Stella and Rachel turned to see what Kirsty was pointing at.

There, in the middle of the goblin
village, above the roofs of the wooden
huts, they could just see the tip of a tall
Christmas tree. Perched on the very top
was a large, silver star. It shimmered
and shone in the cold, grey air. And as
it sparkled, every so often it sent
dazzling darts of silver fairy dust
shooting into the sky.

"It's the Star from the Fairyland Christmas tree!" Stella exclaimed in delight. "You've found it!"

Catch a Falling Star

Rachel, Kirsty and Stella stared up at the Star.

"Quick, let's go and get it right away!" Stella whispered urgently.

As fast as they could, the girls hurried after Stella along the snow-covered track to the centre of the village.

"How will we get the Star down?"

asked Kirsty anxiously.

"Without all those goblins
seeing us!" Rachel added,
stopping dead as she
stared at the scene
ahead of her.

A crowd of grown-
up goblins and
goblin children were
gathered near the
Christmas tree, having
a party. They were all
wrapped up warmly in
hats, scarves and coats.
One was selling hot pies,
and there was a group of
carol-singers holding lanterns.
They were all singing out of tune, just
like the goblin who'd had the magic

GOBLIN GRUB

150

Candle. They sounded so bad that Kirsty wanted to put her hands over her ears! "Goblins aren't very good singers, are they?" she whispered to Rachel. Rachel shook her head. "But they seem to be enjoying themselves," she whispered back, as the goblins launched into another tuneless song. "We have to get the Star down somehow," Stella said thoughtfully. "Girls, if I try to fly up and push the Star off the top of the tree without being spotted, will you try to catch it?"

"Yes, that's a great idea," Rachel said with a grin.

"We'll go and stand under the tree, as close as we can get," Kirsty whispered to Stella. "Good luck!"

Stella zoomed off, and Rachel turned to Kirsty.

"Let's join the party," she said. "But we'd better try and sing out of tune, or they might guess we're not real goblins!"

Putting on their nastiest faces, Rachel
and Kirsty hurried over to join the
carol-singers. None of the goblins gave
them a second glance
as they stood at the
back of the group.
Then the girls
began to sing,
doing their best
to sound flat and
tuneless as they
inched closer to the tree.

"There's Stella!" Kirsty whispered to
Rachel under cover of the loud noise.

Rachel glanced upwards. Stella was
flying high overhead, taking cover behind
the grey clouds. She hovered above the
tree, looking nervously this way and that,
and then began to float downwards.

Suddenly the goblin standing next to Kirsty elbowed her in the ribs. Kirsty almost fell over with fright. Had he noticed Stella?

"You're singing out of tune!" he said with a scowl.

"Sorry!" Kirsty muttered, as gruffly as she could. She decided to sing more quietly.

Rachel could see that Stella had landed on the top of the tree, and was now releasing the Star from the cords which held it. When she was ready, the little fairy waved at Rachel. Carefully, Rachel edged right up to the tree. Then, as Stella pushed the Star gently off the top, Rachel held out her hands.

The Star fell towards her, sparkling as it tumbled through the air. It seemed very bright to Rachel and she was sure one of the goblins would spot it, but to her relief, nobody seemed to notice and she caught it safely before it hit the ground. Quickly she pushed it out of sight beneath her coat, and edged her way back to Kirsty.

"I've got it!" she whispered joyfully.

"Great!" Kirsty beamed.

"What are you whispering about?" snapped the grumpy goblin next to her. He stared curiously at the girls and  they both began to feel quite nervous.

"Do your best grumpy face," Rachel muttered. She and Kirsty pulled their faces into angry frowns, but the goblin didn't stop staring.

"Look!" one of the other carol-singers shouted suddenly. "The Star is missing from the top of the Christmas tree!"

All the goblins looked up at this, and began to mutter angrily as they saw that the Star had gone.

"Where is it?"

"Did it fall off?"

"Who's taken it?"

Then there was another shout from the goblin selling pies. "Look up there!" he cried, pointing towards the top of the tree. "Is that a fairy?"

Run Away!

Rachel and Kirsty stared at each other in horror, then glanced up at Stella. The tiny fairy must have heard the goblin's shout, for she darted quickly out of sight behind one of the large glass baubles hanging on the tree.

Rachel looked down at the front of her coat. To her dismay, she saw that

magical, silvery sparks were shooting
out from between the buttons. "Oh,
no!" she whispered.

The goblin next to Rachel had
noticed the sparks too. He was staring
at them, looking puzzled. He peered at
Rachel's face, and suddenly his face
broke into a frown. "You're not
a goblin!" he hissed, stepping in front
of her. "You've stolen our Star!"

Right at that moment, Kirsty, who was still staring upwards at the tree, suddenly felt her hood slip backwards.

"A girl!" yelled the goblin standing next to her. He was staring at Kirsty as if his eyes were going to pop out. "A human girl!"

"And they've got the Star!" screeched the one who had spotted Rachel.

Rachel pushed past him and grabbed Kirsty's hand. "RUN!" she yelled.

The two girls broke away from the
crowd of goblins, but the goblins
immediately gave chase, shouting
loudly and pushing each other out of
the way. Kirsty looked back at the
tree anxiously, and saw Stella zooming
after them.

"Which way?" Rachel panted, as they
came to a fork in the track.

"This way!" Kirsty took off down the left-hand fork, and Rachel followed. She took a quick glance over her shoulder, and her heart sank. Other goblins were coming out of their houses to see what the noise was about, and they were joining in the chase. Now there were about fifty goblins running after the girls!

"What's going on?" shouted a gruff voice ahead of them. Rachel and Kirsty saw the goblin who had been toasting his toes by the fire, standing in the middle of the track. Like the other goblins, he had heard the noise and come to see what was going on.

"Stop them!" shouted the goblins

behind the girls. "They've stolen the magic Star!" The goblin looked very grave and held up his hand. "STOP!" he roared. But Rachel and Kirsty didn't stop. They dashed past the goblin, one on each side. The goblin was spun round like a spinning-top,

and landed on
his back in
the snow.
"Oh!"
he howled.
"I'm frozen!"

"Come on,
girls!" Stella urged. She had caught up
with Rachel and Kirsty, and now she
hovered over their heads as they ran
down yet another track.

Kirsty was racking her brains, trying to think of an escape plan. If Stella turns us into fairies, we can fly away! she thought, but then she realised that that wouldn't work. The Star was too big for a fairy to carry, and they couldn't leave it behind.

Suddenly, she realised that they were running back into the middle of the village. Both girls slid to a halt by the Christmas tree.

"We've run around in a great big circle!" Rachel groaned in dismay.

"And here come the goblins!" Kirsty panted, her face very pale.

The goblins were rushing towards them from all directions.

"Now we've got you!" one yelled, and the others cheered.

Kirsty turned to Stella. "Stella, if Rachel and I were fairy-sized, do you think the three of us could carry the Star between us?" she asked urgently. "Each of us could hold a corner of it."

"I don't know," Stella replied
doubtfully. "It's quite heavy."

"We'll have to try!" Rachel gasped,
laying the Star carefully on the ground.
"It's our only chance!"

As the goblins surrounded them, Stella
raised her wand.

"There's the Star!" one of the goblins
shouted. "Grab it!"

But before the
goblins could
move, Stella's
magic fairy
dust drifted
over Rachel
and Kirsty.
Immediately the
goblin green faded

away and the girls shrank to fairy-size.

Both girls couldn't help shivering with
fright as they gazed round at the angry
goblins. They looked much bigger and
scarier from a fairy's point of view!

"Quick!" Kirsty shouted, as the circle
of goblins began to close in on them.
"Grab a corner each and fly upwards
as fast as you can!"

Flight to Fairyland

A moment later, Rachel, Kirsty and Stella shot upwards into the sky, lifting the Star with them.

"We've done it!" Rachel cried joyfully.

The goblins below couldn't believe their eyes. They were so surprised, they couldn't stop themselves from colliding

with the Christmas tree, and each
other, as they rushed forwards.
They all bumped their
knobbly knees and
long noses and fell
in a tangled heap
on the ground,
groaning loudly.

"Watch out for
the Christmas
tree!" one of them
shouted warningly.

Hovering high
above the ground,
Stella, Rachel and Kirsty
watched as the huge
Christmas tree tottered and
swayed from side to side. Slowly,
it overbalanced and toppled over.

There were loud shrieks of rage as some of the big goblins were covered with tree branches, tinsel and other decorations, while a group of goblin children who were watching, laughed so hard that *they* fell over too! Stella turned to Rachel and Kirsty, a big smile across her face. "Let's get back to Fairyland right away!" she said. "It's almost nighttime, and Father Christmas will want to start delivering his presents!"

Carrying the Star, Stella, Rachel and
Kirsty flew to Fairyland as fast as their
wings could take them. When they
arrived, they found every single fairy in
the land waiting for them around the
Christmas tree, along with King
Oberon and Queen Titania. All the
fairies gasped with delight as they saw
Stella and the girls flying towards them
with the magic Star.

"The Star!" the fairies shouted excitedly. "Christmas is saved!"

"You are just in time," King Oberon declared, beaming at Stella, Rachel and Kirsty as they flew down to the ground, clutching the Star. "Father Christmas is about to set off on his delivery round!"

"Thank you so much," added Queen Titania gratefully. "Now, would you put the Star back on the tree where it belongs?"

Stella, Rachel and Kirsty flew to the top of the tree and carefully lowered the Star into place.

175

The Star immediately shot dazzling swirls of magic, silver fairy dust from every point, as if it knew it was home again.

"Girls, we all thank you from the bottom of our hearts!" the King declared, as Rachel and Kirsty flew down to stand before him. "We can never repay you fully for your great kindness, but we can promise you an extra special Christmas!"

All of the fairies laughed and clapped, and Kirsty and Rachel looked at each other in delight.

"Thank you for your help, girls," Stella said, kissing them both lightly on the cheek. "And I hope you get everything you want for Christmas!"

"Now, we mustn't keep you any longer," the Queen added. "You have to be home in time to enjoy your own Christmas, after working so hard."

"Merry Christmas, everybody!" Kirsty and Rachel called, as Stella lifted her wand to send them home.

"Merry Christmas!" the fairies
replied. They all waved their wands
in farewell, as Kirsty and Rachel were
swept gently off their feet in a whirl
of sparkling magic.

As the mist of fairy dust faded away,
the girls found themselves back in
Kirsty's snowy back garden. It was
getting dark, and the lights were on in
the Tates' house.

178

"Look!" Rachel pointed up
at the night sky.
"The stars are out."
Kirsty glanced
upwards and saw
with delight that
the stars were
twinkling
brightly like
tiny diamonds.
"What's that
over there?" she
asked Rachel,
pointing at a
large shape moving
swiftly across the sky.
Rachel screwed up her
eyes as she tried to make
out what the shape might be.

"It looks like a sleigh," she said slowly.

Kirsty's eyes opened wide. "It's Father Christmas!" she gasped.

The two girls watched in wonder as Father Christmas's sleigh, pulled by his magic reindeer, zoomed across the sky leaving a trail of golden sparks.

"Oh!" Kirsty cried suddenly. "The golden trail behind the sleigh is spelling out a message!"

Rachel caught her breath, her heart

pounding with excitement. She and Kirsty stared up at the dark night sky, and there against the inky blackness, they could clearly read the words 'Merry Christmas, Rachel and Kirsty!' written in dazzling golden sparks.

As he passed over the Tates' garden, Father Christmas looked down and gave the girls a friendly wave, beaming cheerfully at them. Then the sleigh picked up speed and disappeared behind a cloud.

"He waved at us!" Kirsty laughed. "What a lovely surprise!"

"That was wonderful!" Rachel agreed, her eyes shining as she watched the fiery golden letters fade away into the darkness.

"Girls!" Mrs Tate called from inside the house. "Rachel's parents are here to collect her."

"I think it's going to be a very happy Christmas, Rachel," Kirsty said with a grin, as she and Rachel ran towards the house.

"Yes. Merry Christmas, Kirsty!"
laughed Rachel. "And a merry
Christmas to everyone in Fairyland!"

Win a Rainbow Magic
Sparkly T-Shirt and Goody Bag!

There are seven magic stars in Stella the Star Fairy and each one has a secret letter in it. Find all seven letters and re-arrange them to make a special Fairyland word, then send it to us. Each month we will put the entries into a draw. The winner will receive a Rainbow Magic Sparkly T-shirt and Goody Bag!

Send your entry on a postcard to: Rainbow Magic Stella Competition, Orchard Books, 338 Euston Road, London NW1 3BH. Australian readers should write to Level 17/207 Kent Street, Sydney, NSW 2000. Don't forget to include your name and address. Only one entry per child.

FERN THE GREEN FAIRY
1-84362-019-7

SAFFRON THE YELLOW FAIRY
1-84362-018-9

AMBER THE ORANGE FAIRY
1-84362-017-0

RUBY THE RED FAIRY
1-84362-016-2

HEATHER THE VIOLET FAIRY
1-84362-022-7

IZZY THE INDIGO FAIRY
1-84362-021-9

SKY THE BLUE FAIRY
1-84362-020-0

The Weather Fairies

GOLDIE THE SUNSHINE FAIRY
1-84362-641-1

PEARL THE CLOUD FAIRY
1-84362-635 7

ABIGAIL THE BREEZE FAIRY   1-84362-634-9

CRYSTAL THE SNOW FAIRY   1 84362-633-0

HAYLEY THE RAIN FAIRY
1-84362-638-1

STORM THE LIGHTNING FAIRY
1-84362-637-3

EVIE THE MIST FAIRY
1-84362-636-5

Collect all of the Rainbow Magic books!

The Party Fairies

CHERRY THE CAKE FAIRY
1-84362-818-X

MELODIE THE MUSIC FAIRY
1-84362-819-8

GRACE THE GLITTER FAIRY
1-84362-820-1

HONEY THE SWEET FAIRY
1-84362-821-X

POLLY THE PARTY FUN FAIRY
1-84362-822-8

PHOEBE THE FASHION FAIRY
1-84362-823-6

JASMINE THE PRESENT FAIRY
1-84362-824-4

The Jewel Fairies

INDIA THE MOONSTONE FAIRY
1-84362-958-5

SCARLETT THE GARNET FAIRY
1-84362-954-2

EMILY THE EMERALD FAIRY
1-84362-955-0

CHLOE THE TOPAZ FAIRY
1-84362-956-9

AMY THE AMETHYST FAIRY
1-84362-957-7

SOPHIE THE SAPPHIRE FAIRY
1-84362-953-4

LUCY THE DIAMOND FAIRY
1-84362-959-3

Collect all of the Rainbow Magic books!

by Daisy Meadows

The Jewel Fairies

Coming Soon: The Pet Fairies

All priced at £3.99. *Holly the Christmas Fairy, Summer the Holiday Fairy*
and *Stella the Star Fairy* are priced at £4.99.
Rainbow Magic books are available from all good bookshops, or can be ordered
direct from the publisher: Orchard Books, PO BOX 29, Douglas IM99 1BQ
Credit card orders please telephone 01624 836000
or fax 01624 837033 or visit our Internet site: www.wattspub.co.uk
or e-mail: bookshop@enterprise.net for details.

To order please quote title, author and ISBN and your full name and address.
Cheques and postal orders should be made payable to 'Bookpost plc.'
Postage and packing is FREE within the UK
(overseas customers should add £2.00 per book).
Prices and availability are subject to change.

Have you checked out the

Website at:

www.rainbowmagic.co.uk

There are games, activities and
fun things to do, as well as news
and information about Rainbow
Magic and all of the fairies.